Gabe and Goon

IZA TRAPANI

Charlesbridge

To Gabe, an amazing stepson and the best of friends!
With monstrous hugs, Iza

Published by Charlesbridge
85 Main Street
Watertown, MA 02472
(617) 926-0329
www.charlesbridge.com

Library of Congress Cataloging-in-Publication Data
Trapani, Iza, author, illustrator.
  Gabe and Goon/Iza Trapani.
    pages cm
  Summary: Goon is the monster hiding in Gabe's closet, but the trouble is he is a lot
more afraid of children than Gabe is afraid of monsters.
  ISBN 978-1-58089-640-5 (reinforced for library use)
  ISBN 978-1-60734-866-5 (ebook)
  ISBN 978-1-60734-867-2 (ebook pdf)
1. Monsters—Juvenile fiction. 2. Fear—Juvenile fiction. 3. Friendship—Juvenile fiction.
4. Stories in rhyme. [1. Stories in rhyme. 2. Monsters—Fiction. 3. Fear—Fiction.
4. Friendship—Fiction. 5. Bedtime—Fiction.] I. Title.

PZ8.3.T686Gab 2016
[E]—dc23   2015021182

Printed in Malaysia
(hc) 10 9 8 7 6 5 4 3 2 1

Illustrations done in watercolor, Acryla gouache, Pan pastels, and ink on Arches watercolor paper
Display type set in Baileywicke Festive by Jason Walcott/Jukebox and Tabitha by Chank
Text type set in Italia by Adobe Systems Inc.
Color separations by Colourscan Print Co Pte Ltd, Singapore
Printed by TWP Sdn Bhd in Johor Bahru, Johor, Malaysia
Production supervision by Brian G. Walker
Designed by Diane M. Earley

Gabe wasn't scared of monsters.
He hoped to see one soon.
Well, hiding in his closet
Was a real live monster, GOON.

But **GOON** was scared of children.
He found them odd and kooky.
And when they picked their noses,
They were absolutely spooky.

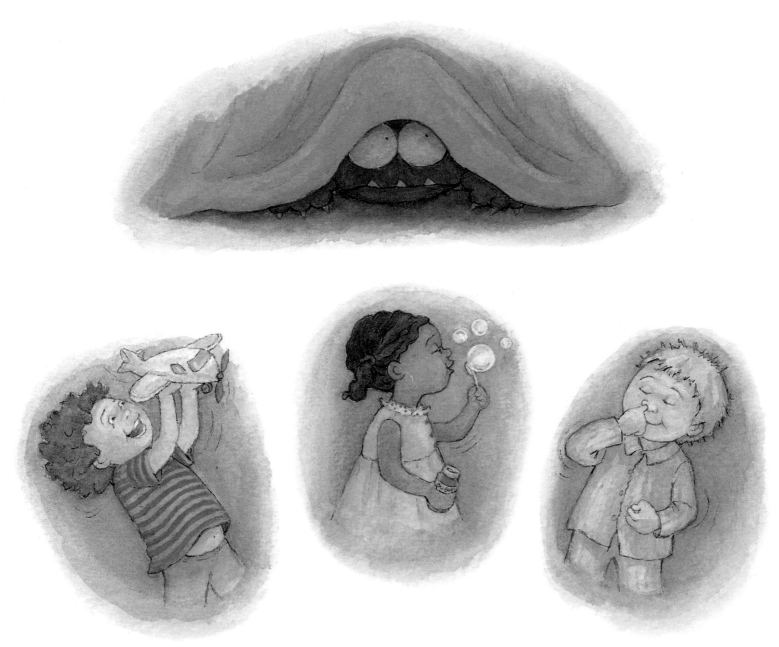

AAAH!

Their horrid little beady eyes,
Their weird and fuzzy hair,
And how they screamed when seeing him
Gave **GOON** an awful scare.

So there inside **Gabe**'s closet,
GOON's heart went pitter-patter.
As **Gabe** was snoring up a storm,
GOON's fangs began to chatter.

Then **Gabe** woke up and blew his nose.
SNORT! HONK! Oh, what a shock!
It sounded like a tuba.
GOON's knees began to knock.

And then **Gabe** sneezed—a huge ACHOO!
It boomed as loud as thunder.
GOON shook so much, the hangers clanged.
And **Gabe** began to wonder . . .

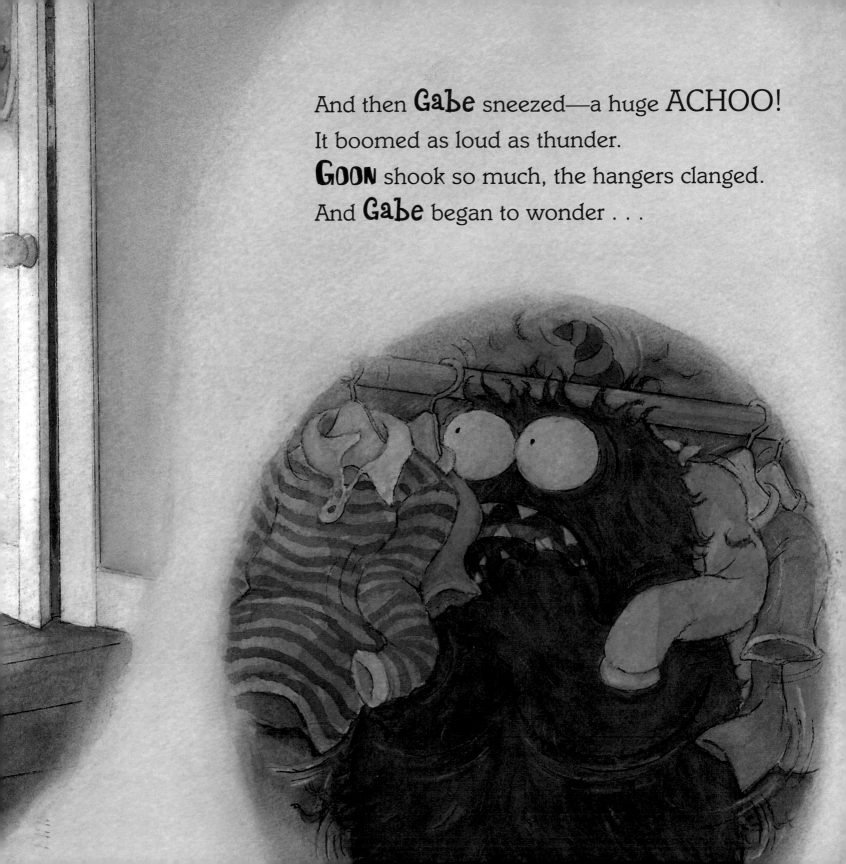

"Is there a monster in my room?
Is this my lucky night?"
Gabe opened up the closet door.
Goon bolted out of sight.

Underneath the bed he hid.
Poor **GOON** was panic-stricken.
"Ha, ha!" **Gabe** mocked. "You're scared of me?
Come out of there, you chicken!"

Now, monsters can be very proud
And easily offended,
And poking fun at them at all
Just isn't recommended.

So **GOON** got brave and made a face,
As gruesome as could be.
But **Gabe** kept right on chuckling,
Saying, "You can't frighten me."

BWA-

GOON then bellowed, "BWA-HA-HA!"
As only monsters can.
Gabe declared, "I'm not afraid.
You'd better try again."

GOON tried a creepy zombie walk
To make himself look meaner.
Gabe said, "You look ridiculous,"
And whooped like a hyena.

GOON stomped his feet and swung his arms
And shook his monster head.
GABE laughed. "You're such a goofball!
You can't scare me," he said.

Just as **GOON** ran out of tricks,
   A spider tiptoed by.
   GOON smiled, then picked it up and said,
"How are you, little guy?"

Gabe shrieked, "Is that a spider?!"
And hid behind the door.
"Get rid of it! I promise
I won't tease you anymore."

Then **GOON** began to giggle.
"Hee, hee! Well, look at that.
You run from little spiders.
Now who's the scaredy-cat?"

Well, children (just like monsters)
Can be offended, too.
But slowly **Gabe** admitted,
"OK, OK, it's true.

"I guess we're not so different.
We both got spooked tonight.
You scared me with that spider,
And I gave you a fright."

So **Gabe** and **GOON** were even,
And as this story ends,
The scaredy-cat and chicken
Became the best of friends.